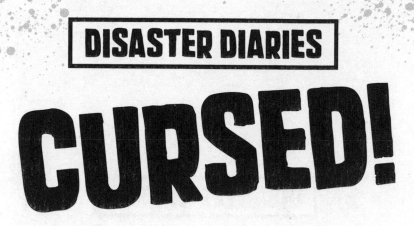

DISASTER DIARIES

CURSED!

DISASTER DIARIES

Zombies!

Aliens!

Brainwashed!

Robots!

Spiders!

Cursed!

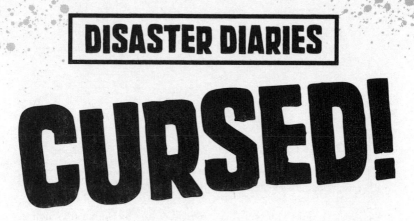

DISASTER DIARIES

CURSED!

R. McGEDDON

⟦Imprint⟧
MAKE YOUR MARK

NEW YORK

Special thanks to Jonny Leighton

[Imprint]
MAKE YOUR MARK

A part of Macmillan Publishing Group, LLC
175 Fifth Avenue, New York, NY 10010

Library of Congress Cataloging-in-Publication Data is available.
ISBN 978-1-250-13567-4 (hardcover) / ISBN 978-1-250-13566-7 (ebook)

Our books may be purchased in bulk for promotional, educational, or
business use. Please contact your local bookseller or the Macmillan
Corporate and Premium Sales Department at (800) 221-7945 ext. 5442 or
by e-mail at MacmillanSpecialMarkets@macmillan.com.

Imprint logo designed by Amanda Spielman

First edition, 2018

10 9 8 7 6 5 4 3 2 1

mackids.com

Read until the final pages,
Or you'll be cursed throughout the ages,
With no one but yourself to thank,
When it's time to walk the plank!

FOR ISAAC . . .

CHAPTER ONE

Three friends wandered through the quiet town of Sitting Duck. The sun was in the sky, the wind was in their faces, and the cheery call of seagulls floated in the air. Happy people waved as they skipped through the streets, and old men cast aside their walkers and danced a merry jig to a whistling tune.

Okay. That's a lie.

Sitting Duck is *fairly* great, but it's not *that* great. Yes, there are dancing old men, obviously, but no, the gulls are not friendly. They'd sooner peck your brain out of your ears or dive-bomb you from above or take you hostage and demand worms and twigs and TVs for their nests and—

Anyway. I'm getting distracted.

Forget the birds for a minute. Instead, remember that three friends were wandering through the town ready for their next adventure. And a young boy named Sam Saunders led the way.

"C'mon, slowpokes!" he cried, with a smile on his face. "We haven't got all day!"

See, if you haven't met Sam, you need to know that he wasn't one for slow *anything*. Sam liked adventure and action and being a hero. When he wasn't playing baseball, he could usually be found fighting off aliens or evil scientists or, most recently, giant spiders that threatened to devour the whole town. So, Sam was all about moving *fast*.

"We're coming!" yelled Arty Dorkins, hitching up his corduroys as he panted and wheezed. Sam's best friend was an all-around genius but not exactly a sports star in the making. In fact, Arty was so clever he had recently made a robot that could talk and think and even do the dishes. This makes it that much more surprising that he didn't remember the belt for his pants this morning.

"But where are we going?" grumbled a third voice. This was Emmie Lane. Emmie was the third action hero and savior of Sitting Duck. She'd battled zombies and creepy critters more often than you've brushed your teeth, let me tell you. (Well, probably. It depends on how often you brush your teeth. It's a very simple equation, though: Teeth Brushing × How Often You Brush Them + Bonus Points for Flossing ÷ Rainbows = the Amount of Zombies and Creepy Critters that Emmie Lane has Faced.) She was loyal and brave and always up for a fight. Although she was a *tiny* bit grumpy and *sometimes* had a bit of a temper. Occasionally. Maybe? (Please don't tell her I said that.)

Anyway, now that the introductions are over, I suppose I should tell you what they were up to. Sam was weaving through the streets, with Arty and Emmie following close behind, still puzzled as to where they were going.

Arty caught the smell of something fishy on the breeze and put two and two together. Sadly, he got fifty-eight, which again, just goes to show . . .

"We're going to the tuna factory, right? Oh man, I've always wanted to visit that place."

"No, we're not," Emmie snapped. "What would we be doing there?"

"Fighting evil tuna that threaten to take over the world with their fishy ways?" Arty suggested.

"Well, maybe," Emmie agreed reluctantly. "Tuna *is* evil. But look, we're going in the wrong direction for the tuna place."

Sam chuckled. They weren't going anywhere near that stinky old factory. Instead, he led them down steep streets and cobbled steps, dodging in and out of warehouses and brick buildings, until they came out onto the Sitting Duck docks. Here, they were buffeted by the sea winds that, yes, had a bit of a fishy tang. But the breeze also carried trumpeting music and the sound of cheery crowds having fun.

Sam stretched out his arms with glee and grinned wildly. "I give you . . . the Founder's Day Festival!"

Arty's face stretched into a grin, but Emmie's face dropped like a bucket down a well. She wasn't really one for community spirit and town celebrations, and the Founder's Day Festival was the biggest one of them all. How could she have forgotten it was this weekend? Every year, the townspeople got together to remember their infamous founder, Armitage Caruthers. They recalled how he'd sailed the seven seas, defeated a mermaid's curse, founded Sitting Duck, and then died a hero, fending off the Great Octopus Invasion of 1675. Arty liked all that historical stuff and Sam *loved* his hero, Armitage Caruthers, but Emmie was less impressed.

"*This* is what you were so excited about?" she asked. "Armitage, the history dude?"

"Yeah, but look!" Sam began. "There's all sorts of cool stuff. Not *just* an amazing local history dude!"

The three friends made their way over to the crowds nestled on the boardwalk, where Sitting Duck's wide Leaky Tap River dribbled its way to the vast Seashell Sea. In the distance, a huge concrete dam reared up, holding back the imaginatively named Lake Deep Puddle. A brass band played jaunty music in front of big fairground rides, and market stalls sold pirate hats in honor of Caruthers and toy ducks in honor of Albertus. (The town founder couldn't afford a parrot, so he had his very own duck pal instead.)

Sam hopped from stall to stall, excited by everything around him. He even played shoot-the-duck and managed to bag himself a stuffed Albertus. He tucked it into his backpack for safekeeping, his eyes bright with glee.

"See," Sam said. "Isn't it awesome?"

Emmie rolled her eyes, bored and unconvinced. Then, just when she thought she couldn't be enjoying the fair less, a big burly man with a tray of drinks squeezed his way past her, splashing her in the process. She was completely soaked.

Founder's Day Festivities

Come one, come all, to the Sitting Duck Founder's Day Festival! Revel in the illustrious history of this swell little town by the sea.* This year's fair features:

- The Time Bender: Ride a roller coaster

that goes so fast it loops back in time and ends before it begins!

- Gory Gary's Ghoulish Ghost Train: Relive Sitting Duck's terrifying past in glorious 3-D. If your pants stay dry, win a prize!

- Coconut Shy: Throw a coconut at a coconut and win a coconut. . . . What's not to love?

- Mystic Pete's Fortune-Telling Feet: Rub Mystic Pete's toes for a glimpse into your future. (Disclaimer: He tells the truth, warts 'n' all!)

*Please ignore any recent zombie infestations, alien attacks, mad-scientist takeovers, robot rampages, and spider invasions. Any such occurrence was a one-time thing.

"Hey, you! Watch where you're going!" she called.

The big burly man turned back. Sam readied himself to help Emmie with some karate-chopping hero work, but surprisingly, the man broke out into a big smile.

"Some grog for ya, young lady?" he offered. Arty cocked his head, watching the server. He thought he had seen him before, somewhere, but he couldn't remember where.

Emmie peered more closely at the tray of drinks. On it, several pint glasses of an amber liquid tottered about, frothing and fizzling all over the place. I wouldn't have touched that stuff with a very long stick, let alone drank it, but then, what do I know? (Well, actually quite a lot, because I am the one telling the story.)

"Erm . . ." Emmie hesitated. "What is it?"

"Just some fizzy soda from ye olde pirate days," the man said brightly. "Tasty, too."

Emmie glanced around. It did look like everyone else in Sitting Duck was getting into the spirit, slurping down the festive mixture. So, she bravely withheld her reservations about Founder's Day and joined the fun, taking a sip of the amber fizz, as Sam also reached for a glass.

In an instant, her face tensed and her cheeks went as red as a sailor's belly. Her curly hair stood straight, and she spat out the liquid all over the ground.

"YOWZERS!" she yelled. "That stuff is *gross*."

"Oh," said Sam, withdrawing his hand and laughing. "In that case, let's avoid it, eh, Arty?"

11

"Good idea, I'd say, Sam," Arty chimed in.

Emmie glowered at them, and Sam and Arty suddenly studied their feet, shamefaced. Funny how the boys let *her* try it first—not very friendly if you ask me!

Anyhow, before she had a chance to say anything, a loud call echoed out from the bandstand. Sam's dad, Mayor Saunders, stood on stage, framed by a bright blue background drape, ready to make a speech.

"Ladies and gentlemen," he began, "welcome to the three-hundred-and-fiftieth Sitting Duck Founder's Day!"

A cheer went up from the crowd. Sam spotted all his favorite townspeople, from old Mrs. Missus to seven-foot Sheila. Everyone was in fine spirits, drinking the disgusting grog and hanging on the mayor's every word.

Mayor Saunders continued. "And because it's a special occasion and a milestone in the history of our town, we've got a surprise. . . ."

A whisper of excitement rippled through the crowd. Mr. Saunders stepped aside and a man in a dark suit stepped up on the stage. Mr. Tweedy was his name, and he looked a bit tweedy by nature, too—he had a fancy mustache and wore a dashing bow tie. As the local museum's curator, Tweedy was a known figure 'round old Sitting Duck, too. He was often at the town meetings, during one catastrophe or another, trying to get residents to learn the lessons of history. When the aliens came, he thought they would have learned from the zombies; when the mad scientist came, he thought they would have learned from the aliens.

But sadly, the townsfolk never listened, nor did they help the situations at hand. If anything, they made the disasters more disastrous.

Tweedy approached the microphone, puffed out his chest, and smiled so brightly that several residents shielded their eyes.

"Sitting Duckers!" he bellowed, his wild hair dancing in the wind. "It gives me great pleasure to be in the heart of our magnificent town with you all today."

A loud roar went up from the crowd in approval. The charismatic figure had the audience in the palm of his hand. Until he started speaking again.

"Despite how useless our town is . . ."

A few murmurs went up from the crowd.

"Despite the cowardly nature of its inhabitants . . ."

A few yells went up from the crowd.

"And despite inflicting terrifying, apocalyptic forces upon ourselves every now and then . . ."

A few bottles went flying from the crowd.

"We've survived three hundred and fifty years!" he said with a flourish, rescuing himself from the increasingly angry audience. "So, I present to you, fully restored and the pride of Sitting Duck for another three hundred and fifty years: the original *Silver Mallard*!"

The residents looked at one another in confusion. Old Mrs. Missus's eyebrows scrunched up in uncertainty. She was sure she'd heard that name somewhere. . . .

Mr. Tweedy realized that nobody in Sitting Duck had been paying attention at his recent Sitting Duck History exhibition whatsoever.

"Eh-hem . . . That's to say, the giant ship that brought our founder to these shores . . ."

Suddenly, the crowd understood, and there was a collective (and very dramatic) gasp. Sam did a double take. *Could it really be Armitage Caruthers's ship? Sailing once more?*

With a flourish, Mr. Saunders swept the blue drapes aside, and the ship was revealed in all its glory. Now, the residents *really* remembered. Previously, the ship had been a wreck, but the Sitting Duck historical smarties had obviously worked hard to restore it to its former glory. Now it stood proudly in the dock, masts standing tall and sails puffed in the wind.

"Wow!" Sam gasped, amazed.

A cannonball fizzed from the ship. Then another. And another. The crowd went wild as the ship fired in salute of Sitting Duck, and Sam looked on as if all his pirating hero dreams had come true at once.

"So much for Founder's Day being boring, eh, Emmie?" he laughed.

Emmie just smiled. "I suppose it's finally gone off with a bang!"

CHAPTER TWO

Sam tossed and turned like a ship in a restless sea. Suddenly, something punched him in the face and snapped him to attention.

"Yargh!" he yelled, ready to fight off a zombie horde or a bunch of evil spiders. But it wasn't either of those; instead, it was an alarm clock shaped just like CHARLES, Arty's robot friend. (Remember, the one from book four who was happy doing the dishes until he tried to destroy everyone?) Only now he was teeny tiny and all he did was smack you in the face when you needed to wake up.

Sam rubbed his nose and sat upright, remembering where he was. After the festival, his mom and dad had let him stay over at Arty's house. All night they'd pretended to be pirates out on the high seas, riding the *Silver Mallard* galleon ship and sailing all over the world.

Sam sighed. It'd been a while since his last adventure, and he thought it was about time for another one.

Quickly, CHARLES the alarm clock scuttled across the floor, leaped up onto Arty's bed, and jabbed him in the face.

"Doughnuts! Candy apples! Cake!" Arty shouted as he woke. (No prizes for guessing what was on *his* mind when he was dreaming.) "Um, morning, Sam," he said, trying to act casual.

"Morning, Arty," Sam said. "Want to get some breakfast?"

Arty literally jumped at the idea, hopping out of bed and into his slippers. The two of them didn't waste any time running downstairs and scooting across the hallway to Arty's kitchen.

Arty was a master breakfasteer (a term that means "one who holds encyclopedic knowledge of all types of breakfast"), so he took great pleasure in listing all the sugary breakfasts they could enjoy. "So we've got pancakes, normal cake, that cereal with the stars and moons, bread, jam, double jam, double bubble jam . . ."

Arty continued in this manner for quite some time, until he stopped, very abruptly.

"That's weird," he said slowly.

"What?" asked Sam. "The forty-five different varieties of breakfast we could have?"

"No," said Arty. "What's weird is that no one's here. Where is everyone?"

Arty looked around in confusion. The

Dorkinses were early risers and quick eaters—and though none of them was the breakfasteer that Arty was, it wasn't like them to miss the first meal of the day.

"Dunno," said Sam. "Catastrophic time-travel disaster? Apocalyptic vampire werewolves?"

"Hmm," Arty thought aloud, rubbing his chin. "That's all very possible, but it wouldn't mean that they'd miss breakfast. . . ."

As if on cue, though, the familiar booming voice of his brother echoed from the living room.

"Ah," Arty said. "There's Jesse. He must've just been sleeping in. . . ."

He and Sam went to see what Jesse was up to, and they nearly fell down with fright.

"Yargh!" Arty yelled when he encountered his brother.

Arty's normally good-looking and annoying older brother, Jesse, was covered in bright green spots. He looked like an alien crossed with a frog crossed with something that crawled out from a sewer in your wildest nightmare. Arty leaped back in shock.

"I think I'm sick, little dweebs," Jesse said, coughing feebly and declaring a statement of the incredibly obvious. "Wh-what's up?"

"Your face!" Sam said. "There's definitely something up with your face."

"Nothing's wrong with my face. I just have a cough," Jesse said, puzzled.

"Erm, you might want to check on that," said Arty.

Jesse stumbled over to a mirror and nearly choked. He obviously hadn't checked his

reflection yet this morning—a rare occurrence—
so after one look at his spotty face he ran
shrieking from the room like the ghoul he now
somewhat resembled. "I'm a monster!" he yelled.
"A monnsterrr!"

"That's weird," said Sam.

"I know," Arty agreed. "He's always been a monster. Has he just realized it now?"

"I don't mean that!" Sam said. "I mean I've never seen anything like those green spots before. They're like radioactive chicken pox!"

Arty didn't seem too worried. If Jesse was ill, it meant that he'd get a break from his older brother being a jerk. And if his mom and dad were still in bed, it meant that he and Sam could eat as much double jam and triple peanut butter as they wanted and then head outside to play baseball in the park.

However, when they finished their breakfast and made their way through Sitting Duck, they couldn't help noticing other ill people as well. Apart from just having gross green spots, a couple of people had muscle spasms. They passed old

Mrs. Missus, who looked like she was doing a pirate jig. Seven-foot Sheila looked like she was waltzing and tap-dancing at the same time. All in all, the residents of Sitting Duck did not look hot.

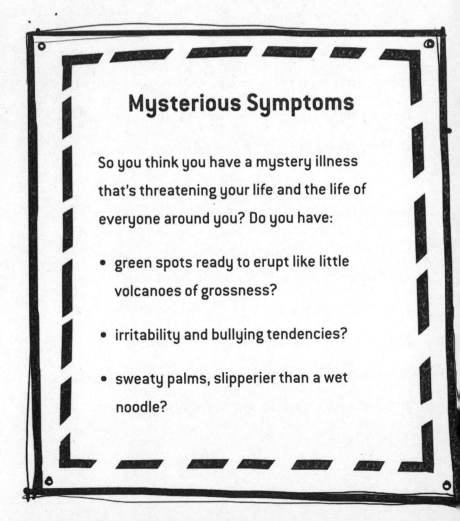

Mysterious Symptoms

So you think you have a mystery illness that's threatening your life and the life of everyone around you? Do you have:

- green spots ready to erupt like little volcanoes of grossness?

- irritability and bullying tendencies?

- sweaty palms, slipperier than a wet noodle?

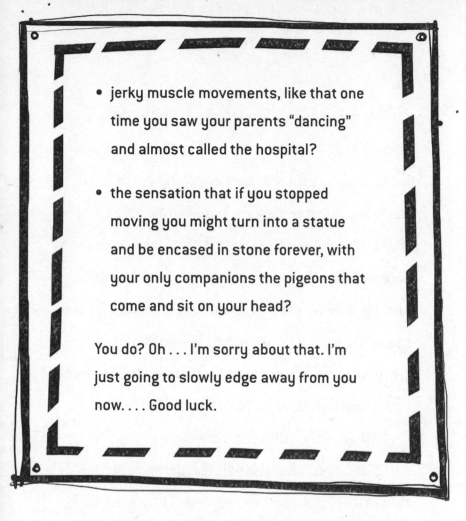

- jerky muscle movements, like that one time you saw your parents "dancing" and almost called the hospital?

- the sensation that if you stopped moving you might turn into a statue and be encased in stone forever, with your only companions the pigeons that come and sit on your head?

You do? Oh . . . I'm sorry about that. I'm just going to slowly edge away from you now. . . . Good luck.

Soon, they made it to the park and waited at the steel gates, their usual spot. Only a couple of minutes later, Emmie came rushing around the corner, Phoebe Bowles in tow.

"Hey, Emmie," Sam laughed, "brought a friend?"

Emmie grumbled. Somehow, however hard she tried, Emmie never seemed to be able to shake Phoebe despite the fact that they were complete opposites: Emmie was an action star, and Phoebe was the primmest girl you could ever meet. This time, Phoebe had brought along her Chihuahua, Glitterpuff, who yapped and growled approximately every thirty seconds.

"Apparently," Emmie huffed.

"Have you, like, seen all the gross people in this town?" Phoebe interrupted. "They seriously need a Makeover Monday. What's with all the spots?"

Sam was about to reply when his nose was assaulted by Phoebe's overpowering scent. It was like a cosmetic shop made of oranges and limes and lemons had exploded all over her. She was practically a one-woman fruit bowl.

"Urm, I don't know," he managed, gasping for fresh air. "But I'm beginning to think something bad is going down."

"I agree," Emmie said. "Even Great Aunt Doris is ill. And she hasn't had so much as a sniffle since the Great Goose Flu Panic of 1935."

Sam nodded thoughtfully. Things were looking strange for the young Sitting Duckers— something was definitely amiss. It wasn't just Sam's nose that was tingling; it was his hero sensors as well.

As if on cue, a whirring noise like an angry metallic cat screeched overhead. Glitterpuff barked hysterically and ran in circles. The kids looked up and saw a huge helicopter dashing above them. Then it was followed by another, and another. Back down below, an ambulance scrambled past, and a huge khaki-green army truck raced behind it followed by a host of other emergency services vehicles. Sam, Arty, and Emmie looked at one another with a mix of horror and excitement.

"What's going on?" Emmie cried.

"I don't know," said Sam. "But we're going to find out!"

They packed up their things and raced after the convoy heading to the center of town. Phoebe snatched up Glitterpuff and darted after them.

"Wait for me," she cried. "My yoga

class starts in five

minutes. . . ."

But Sam, Arty, and
Emmie didn't care about yoga. They'd
had enough saving-the-day experience to
know that something bad was afoot. (To clarify,
afoot means "happening." Not the actual five-toed
foot at the end of your leg. All right. Moving on.)
Sam led them through the streets, crossing under
bridges and hopping over walls, intercepting the
convoy of ambulances and army trucks at every
turn.

"They're heading to the hospital," he cried as a
helicopter whooshed overhead. "This way!"

As they reached the outskirts of the huge
hospital complex, they saw that the whole place
was a hive of activity. The entire parking lot had

been covered with giant plastic tents in bright colors. Cops and doctors swarmed around like angry bees and army personnel strutted their stuff. Helicopters landed and took off with alarming speed, and green army jeeps piled into view. Sam could smell the scent of disinfectant wafting on the breeze.

"Whoa!" said Arty. "I haven't seen Sitting Duck mobilize like this since . . . ever!"

"It looks like disease control of some sort," Emmie guessed, eyeing the medical supplies. "What if there's another outbreak of Goose Flu? I'm not ready to start growing feathers!"

"In that case, we need to figure out what's happening," said Sam. "And fast!"

Sam, Arty, and Emmie edged forward to where the army convoys had screeched to a halt and medical tents had been set up. Phoebe, bewildered, clutched Glitterpuff tight. Almost immediately, a gruff-looking soldier with a jaw like a shovel stopped them in their tracks.

"No entry, kids," he barked.

"But . . . what's going on?" Sam asked.

"That is classified information. Civilians will be informed if necessary."

Sam stepped back. He wasn't about to take that lying down. He was about to take that standing up and sneaking around. He gave the soldier a friendly salute and yanked the others away.

"This way!" he whispered.

Because Sitting Duck had a bad habit of being useless in the face of a crisis, the whole place was in chaos. Together, they skirted the edges of the cordon and moved away from where the bulk of the soldiers were to find themselves a quiet spot. The place was lined with police tape, but the kids easily ducked that and made their way into the tented area.

"What are we doing?" Phoebe moaned. "I need to get to yoga!"

Emmie shushed her as they crept alongside one of the giant plastic tents.

"Look," Sam said. "In there."

The four kids peered around the opening of the tent. Inside, a laboratory was set up with a lot of complex equipment whirring away. Right in the center of the space, three people in bright yellow hazmat suits spoke in hushed tones. They looked like canaries about to go on a space mission. The kids leaned in farther to hear them talk.

"It's spreading like double jam on toast," the first guy said. "There's nothing we can do to stop it."

"And we don't even know what it is," the other replied. "If we don't find a cure, Sitting Duck is doomed!"

CHAPTER THREE

Sam, Arty, and Emmie looked at one another in alarm. As if they didn't have enough to worry about, what with homework and school and brushing their teeth *twice* a day. (Frankly, that seems a little excessive to me.) Now they had to deal with *another* Sitting Duck problem, or the town wouldn't survive to see its 351st anniversary.

Then, right on cue, like the annoying ball of glittery fur that he was, Glitterpuff decided to start yapping and make things a whole lot worse.

"No, my little prince of loveliness, be quiet!" Phoebe tried.

But it was no good. Glitterpuff had something to say, and he wanted to say it. I mean, I don't know exactly what he said because I don't understand Tiny Dog. (Large Dog is a different story. I'm fluent.) It went something like:

"Bark, bark, woof, barkety-bark!"

Phoebe tried to shush him again, but it was too late. The barking pup caused just enough of a ruckus to alert the scientists in their bright yellow hazmat suits. They came rushing from the tent like spacemen running for an intergalactic bus.

"Hey, kids! You're not supposed to be here!"

Sam and friends didn't waste any time hanging around. They've had a lot of practice with escaping, running, fleeing, etc. As the scientists reached for them, they dodged the scientists and sprinted out of the tent and through the hospital cordon. After they'd safely lodged themselves in some bushes for camouflage, they made sure the scientists weren't following them and then hunkered down to try and figure out what to do.

"That Chihuahua of yours nearly got us caught!" Emmie hissed.

"Woof," he barked but sadly the children also don't speak Tiny Dog, so they ignored his apology.

"I'm sorry!" Phoebe said. "But he never listens to me. It's like we speak different languages."

It was exactly like that.

"Never mind," Sam said. "We need answers. Let's go to the Town Hall. My dad will be there, and he can tell us all about what's going on."

The kids untangled themselves from the bushes with only a couple hundred thorns in

So, You're Learning to Speak Dog

There comes a time in every human's life that communicating with a dog is necessary. You might not be able to bark fluently, but it's easy to read your pet's body language. Keep this handy guide on file for all your pet-talking needs:

- Wags tail: "I'm so happy! Happy, happy, happy!"

- Sniffs the ground: "Do I smell a squirrel? Or another dog? Or a cat? Or a person? Or you? Or me? Or nothing?"

- Lies on the ground and rolls around: "My back itches."

- Points ears up and holds head high: "IS THAT A SQUIRREL?! WHAT IS THAT? I HOPE THAT'S A SQUIRREL!"

- Sits in a chair, smokes a pipe, and reads the newspaper: "I am not a dog."

Disclaimer: Scientific accuracy unproven

their butts and made their way across town again. They passed several more green-spotted individuals, looking pale and unwell, and shuddered. Whatever it was, the illness had gained ground.

Reaching the Town Hall, they bounded up the steps. Instead of going through the door, they went straight through the giant hole in the side. (Sitting Duck has been through a lot. Not all buildings have fancy decorations like *walls* and *doors*, you know.) When inside, they ran up the stairs to the mayor's room and bumped right into Sam's dad.

"Oh, hello," said Mr. Saunders, with a broad smile on his face. "What brings you here?"

"Haven't you seen what's going on?" Sam asked. "The whole town is in chaos."

Mr. Saunders popped his head out of the window and noticed the people wandering around like headless hamsters. He then peered around the office, where a team of plastic-suited health officials sprayed down his belongings with chemicals.

"Oh yes," he said. "I thought there was something different around town today."

Sam despaired. Sometimes adults had about as much sense as a talking Chihuahua. He spotted a TV in the corner of the office and reckoned a bit of Live Action News would show his dad just how serious things were.

"Look!"

He flicked the switch and up popped Jock McGarry, Sitting Duck's answer to a question nobody asked. He wore a snazzy black suit, had a mustache that jiggled across his top lip like a particularly hairy worm, and a dazzling smile that was so shiny it could be used as a spotlight. McGarry had presented the news for as long as anybody could remember, except he never got it exactly right. When the zombie hordes attacked, he dismissed it as a spot of nasty weather.

Right now, he was doing a special report from outside the hospital. Doctors ran behind him in panic. Nurses wielded strange medical instruments. And all of them had deadly looking green spots covering their faces. McGarry pulled one person aside for an interview.

"Nasty cold you got there, sonny," he began. "What is it? A flu?"

The green-spotted doctor grabbed McGarry by the striped tie, panic seared across his face. "It's the worst contagion I've ever seen in my life!" he yelled. "This is the end of Sitting Duck. It could be the end of mankind. We're cursed, gosh darn it all. *CURSED!*"

Then the doctor's face stilled. His limbs began to shake, and his arms shot up into the air. It was like he was doing a bad dance at a wedding or a rowdy pirate jig. His body stopped jerking, and there was a puff of gray smoke. As the smoke faded, it revealed the doctor, his skin now turned gray and his body completely frozen.

McGarry looked back to the camera, away from the man still frozen beside him. "So, as you can see, it's all a fuss about nothing folks, just like those fun alien guys and those cuddly spider critters. . . ."

Unbeknownst to McGarry, a great big green spot had just appeared on the end of his nose.

Sam switched off the TV. "See!" he said. "McGarry thinks it's fine. So it must be a catastrophe!"

This seemed to snap Sam's dad to attention. Mr. Saunders puffed out his chest and straightened his tie. "By the ghost of zombies past and present, I think you're right!" he shouted.

He sprang into action. Sam had never seen his dad act so decisively. Mr. Saunders yanked the penholder in the middle of his desk, as if it were a lever. The entire desk flipped upside down, exposing a small glass box containing a big red button.

"Get to safety, kids. I'm activating Emergency Protocol 54-F/Geronimo," Mr. Saunders boomed. "Oh, and you should cover your ears."

"But what about you, Dad?" Sam asked.

Sam's dad took off his tie and wrapped it around his forehead. He looked off into the distance and put on his best action-hero voice. "It's my duty to stay here and protect this town, son, just like all the other times it's faced danger."

Sam, Arty, and Emmie looked at one another, eyebrows raised. They couldn't remember exactly when Mr. Saunders had helped them save the town when it was being overrun by the past five disasters.

"Now go!" he said.

Mr. Saunders slammed his fist down on the glass box, shattering it, and thumped the red button. For a moment, there was stillness, but then an alarm rang out that could have reawakened the dinosaurs. Sam hesitated, but the others yanked him away.

"He'll be fine!" Arty said.

"Yeah," Emmie agreed. "He clearly has that hero vibe the same as you!"

Sam supposed they were right. He nodded, and the four of them sprinted out of there as fast as their little legs could manage.

"Where are we going, guys?" Emmie asked as they ran out into the street.

"Just follow me," said Arty. "I've been preparing for this moment all my life. . . ."

Sam, Emmie, and Phoebe were puzzled but had no other choice than to follow Arty. Thousands of residents swarmed about in the streets, all terrified by the high-pitched emergency alarm that was blaring through the town. Sam hadn't seen a crush like it since Phoebe Bowles fell in love with Arty's brother. No, seriously, though. By *crush*, I mean a LOT of people all piling into one another. There are multiple meanings of the word *crush*, you know. Look it up if you don't believe me.

The kids grabbed one another's hands and formed a human chain to keep themselves from being swept away by the tide of spotted residents, all shaking with illness. Whatever the disease was, it had firmly taken over Sitting Duck.

"Hold on tight, guys," said Arty as he led the way.

Sam felt his grip loosen on Phoebe. Several twitching townsfolk crushed against them, and he only just managed to hold on. Phoebe began to twist and turn, and Sam realized she was actually trying to get away from him.

"What are you doing?" he yelled. "We've got to get to safety!"

"You don't understand," she replied. "I'm going to be *really* late for yoga. . . ." Sam tried to keep hold, but it was no use. Phoebe ripped her hand free and took off in the other direction.

"No! Come back—" Sam began, but it was no use. Phoebe's love of stretching like a clown's balloon was going to get her ill. Or worse. (Cue the dramatic music; I suggest the theme from the 1986 classic *Horror in the Hair Salon*. It has a lovely beat.)

He felt a tugging on his other arm, as Emmie dragged him in the other direction. Something told him she was less bothered to see Phoebe go.

They scuttled their way out through the crush and into a side street to catch their breath.

"So what now, big brain?" Emmie asked. "How do we survive this one?"

Arty smiled and said three words. "Awesome. Emergency. Bunker!"

CHAPTER FOUR

In a little corner of Sitting Duck sat Arty
Dorkins's house. And behind that house was
a garden as boring as you could imagine:
grass, shed, tree—all pleasant and proper. But,
underneath that garden, below the soil and the
worms and the buried secrets and the hidden
treasure, was a surprise bigger than them all.

"This way!" Arty yelled. "Help me find it. . . ."

Sam, Arty, and Emmie crouched down on the
grass. He told them they were looking for a daisy.
But not just any daisy. This daisy had yellow
leaves and a white center, instead of white leaves
and a yellow center. It was one in a million, but if
they found it, they'd be saved. Arty had made it

unique for security purposes, but as it turned out, it was quite hard to locate in a crisis.

After several minutes of scanning the ground, Sam clenched his fist in delight. "Got it!" he cried. You see, he wasn't a hero for nothing.

Arty rushed over and examined the tiny flower. "That's it, all right," he said. "Stand back."

Arty tugged at the daisy and something amazing happened. Because it wasn't just a normal daisy, oh no! Instead, it was a switch. And when Arty pulled the switch, the ground gave way and a set of stairs appeared from nowhere.

"Holy smokes!" Sam cried. "What is this thing?"

"This is where we wait out the end of the world," Arty said proudly.

Sam, Arty, and Emmie barreled down the

stairs until they reached a giant steel door. Arty punched in the code, did a pirouette, picked his nose, stuck out his tongue, and counted backward down from ten in French.

"It's a very sophisticated lock system," he explained.

A loud *bleep* sounded from the lock, and then the steel door swung open. A whoosh of air thwacked them in the face, and the kids rushed inside the mysterious bunker, the door shutting behind them with a dull thud.

Sam and Emmie both stared, wide-eyed.

"WHOA!" they said in unison.

What they saw was pretty cool, I have to admit. I've seen my fair share of emergency end-of-the-world bunkers (in fact, I'm in one right now—top-secret location, obviously), but the one

Arty had created topped them all.

It had concrete walls and steel beams to keep it safe from attack, and it contained all the survival necessities anyone could need, including food, beds, water, Ping-Pong tables, and a lifetime supply of smooth peanut butter.

"Where was this place when the aliens attacked and the spiders were trying to kill us?" Emmie asked.

"Well, it took a while to build . . . ," Arty admitted.

"And besides," Sam continued, "this is a temporary measure, right? Once we get a handle on the situation, we're going to save Sitting Duck like always. We're heroes, remember."

Emmie and Arty nodded. They were good kids like that—always up for an adventure.

Emergency Bunker

Have you ever wanted your own emergency bunker for a potential disaster in your town? Well, want no more! The bunker could be yours in just four small steps. Check out the special features in Arty's bunker for inspiration:

- Twelve-inch-thick walls to survive nuclear blasts, atomic ants, and burrowing badgers. (Burrowing badgers are a menace.)

- A laser detection system to blast anything that comes within a ten-mile radius. (A couple of laser pens and a battery should do the trick.)

- A giant tropical fish tank for maximum dramatic impact. (Also, potential food supply?) Why not make your Emergency

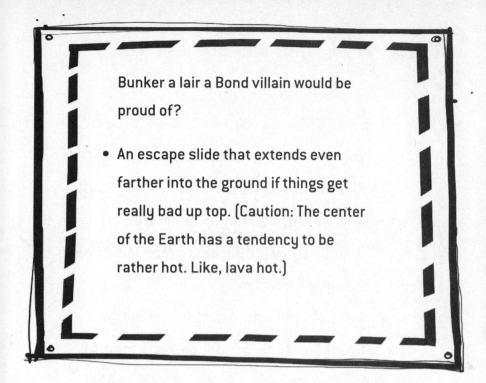

Bunker a lair a Bond villain would be proud of?

- An escape slide that extends even farther into the ground if things get really bad up top. (Caution: The center of the Earth has a tendency to be rather hot. Like, lava hot.)

Arty led them over to a bank of computer screens. They showed maps of Sitting Duck and real-time coverage of what was happening across the town. Green blobs dotted around the screen, monitoring the disease. It was obvious that the thing was spreading like wildfire; soon the whole town would be taken over, maybe even the world.

"This thing is horrible," Sam moaned.

"Pfft," said Emmie. "It would take more than a green blobby disease to incapacitate me."

"Well, it managed with everyone else," said Arty. "And we still don't know what it is."

"I'll handle it," said Emmie firmly. "Just point me in the right direction."

As well as being reinforced with nuclear-attack-proof steel and having enough food to last them a seriously long time, Arty's bunker had a full library. Emmie went down a corridor and found herself in a plush wood-paneled room, complete with an open fireplace and leather armchairs.

"Yeesh," she said to herself. "Maybe the end of the world isn't so bad after all."

She scanned the shelves and plucked out a volume that looked interesting: *Dr. Cadaver's*

Morbus Liber: *Diseases, Sneezes, and Bacteria-Carrying Weasels*. It promised to chronicle every disease known to man or beast, so Emmie lugged the bricklike book to a table and got to work.

She flicked through the index and tried to find the symptoms she already knew: green spots on the face and weird, jerky body movements like a pirate jig. She ran her fingers down the myriad entries and got excited when she discovered one that looked just right: Jumping Toad Fever.

"'Jumping Toad Fever,'" she read out loud. "'Symptoms: green spots, jerky body movements. Ends with patient's skin turning to slime. Cure: bucket of salt and a warm bath.'"

Emmie frowned—the last symptom of Jumping Toad Fever didn't seem quite right. She read out the next entry.

"'Green Apple Coughing Tree,'" Emmie began. "'Symptoms include: green spots, jerky body movements. Ends when the victims cough up just enough apples to make a delicious sauce—goes lovely with a nice side of pork!'"

"Arghh . . . ," Emmie grumbled. "That's not it, either."

Suddenly, she heard a noise from the other room. It sounded like Sam was cheering. She raced back through the bunker's corridors to the main room, where she found Sam punching the air.

"Have you found out something?" she gasped. "What is it?"

Sam looked sheepish.

"Erm, no. I just beat Arty at Ping-Pong," he said, gently putting down the paddle on the table and moving backward away from Emmie.

Emmie exploded. I mean, not literally, but still. Good thing the bunker was bombproof, fireproof and volcanoproof, because Emmie lit up like a mixture of all three.

"Have you not noticed we've got a town to save?" she blared.

Arty and Sam looked ashamed and followed Emmie into the bunker's library to bury their noses in a couple of books for a few hours. Sadly for Sam, Emmie noticed what he was reading and was even less impressed. In his hands was a leather-bound version of *Armitage Caruthers: Tales from the High Seas*. While Emmie had

been researching diseases, Sam had been in an historical world of heroes and villains.

"And what is that?" she demanded, snatching at the book. (Honestly . . . you don't want to get on the wrong side of Emmie. Didn't I tell you she has a temper?)

Sam protested. "It's research, too! I just got distracted." He snatched the book back and held it aloft so Emmie couldn't reach it.

"In fact," he said, with a note of triumph in his voice, "I think I've found something."

He excitedly flipped the pages. The book described Armitage Caruthers's journey across the Atlantic, the different pirates he fought, and the storms that lashed the ship along the way. But the most important part was about the *Silver Mallard*, the ship that Caruthers and his men were sailing in, and the one that Mayor Saunders and Mr. Tweedy from the museum had restored for Sitting Duck's 350th birthday celebrations.

"'A mysterious disease wiped out the crew, leaving the ship in grave danger,'" Sam read. "'Strange green spots appeared on the men, for which no known reason could be imagined. . . .'"

Arty and Emmie looked at each other in alarm.

Sam swelled to the big finish. "'There could be but one explanation,'" he read. "'The *Silver Mallard* was cursed!'"

CHAPTER FIVE

Arty and Emmie burst into spasms of laughter. They heaved up and down like bouncy castles letting out all their air at once, their guffaws echoing around the concrete bunker.

"A curse?" Arty scoffed. "You do know there's no such thing, right?"

"That's basically *magic*," Emmie added. "It's right up there with witches and broomsticks and goblins and friendly teachers. They don't exist!"

Sam's face turned pink. He didn't like being told he was wrong, especially when it was about his hero, Armitage Caruthers, and the founding of Sitting Duck.

"It's true," he said desperately, reading the story out loud. "Listen to this."

According to the legend, Armitage Caruthers and his men had found a lost island in the middle of the Atlantic. It wasn't on any of the maps, but it was covered in tall trees with emerald-green leaves and beautiful white sandy beaches. So, desperate for supplies, Armitage and his men decided to use it as a stopping point in their long journey.

But what they found surprised them. On the rocky coast of the northern side of the island, there were caves and tunnels filled with treasure beyond their wildest dreams. We're talking gold and rubies piled in heaps, crowns with diamonds encrusted in them, and swords with silver handles. The pirates thought that all their

holidays—and birthdays and double rainbows—
had come at once.

So, they set about loading as much of the
golden treasure on board as they possibly could.
The sailors worked day and night to clear out
the caves and pile all the goodies onto the *Silver
Mallard*. But what they didn't know was that the
treasure belonged to mermaids and mermen—
but remember, everyone, merfolk are evil. The
merfolk knew all about the thieving sailors—
in fact Armitage Caruthers had once been
imprisoned by the queen of the merfolk herself
for impersonating a monkfish. So, they'd placed
a curse upon the jewels. Anyone who touched the
treasure of would be cursed for all eternity. Ugly
green spots like precious emeralds would appear
on their faces, they'd dance uncontrollably like

the unruly pirates that they were, and, finally, they would turn to stone. The curse would spread, and no one would be spared.

Once Caruthers realized the jewels were cursed, he was left with no choice but to leave the treasure untouched on the boat. Even when he finally sailed into Sitting Duck Port, the men weren't allowed to take it with them.

"The mermaids and mermen called the curse the 'Sailor's Sleep'!" Sam finished breathlessly. "When Tweedy and his men restored the ship, they must have unleashed the curse once again!"

This time, Arty and Emmie didn't laugh. Even though it sounded like a wild tale the likes of which they'd never heard before, the curse *did* sound like the disease that was spreading around Sitting Duck. And it did happen just after the *Silver Mallard* arrived, newly restored, in the Sitting Duck docks. If it were true, then they were dealing with something much scarier than what Emmie found in *Dr. Cadaver's* Morbus Liber, something that the world had not seen in hundreds of years.

Suddenly, a loud *BLEEP* broke the silence. They rushed over to see to Arty's flashing and whirring computer system. Arty pored over the data and system messages.

"The disease has peaked, and the infection level is falling," Arty cried. "It looks like it's safe to go outside."

The three friends looked at one another. If they stayed inside, they could play Ping-Pong and stay nice and warm by the fire, no problemo. But, of course, they weren't those kind of kids. They all knew it was time to get ready to ship out.

"Whatever we find out there," said Sam, "we'll face it together."

Sam picked up his backpack and shoved his baseball bat in there. Emmie gathered her things and ripped a couple of pages out of the medical book to take with her. Arty, good old Arty, he ran and got the one thing that mattered most: his Swiss Barmy Knife.

"What *is* that?" Emmie asked.

"Oh, this?" Arty said proudly. "It's like an army knife, but it's a barmy knife. It has every possible attachment you could think of: a knife, a spoon, keys, a lollipop, a feather duster . . ."

Emmie zoned out as Arty continued to list all the useless things on his so-called "knife." Sam snapped them both to attention.

"Let's get out of here, guys—we haven't got all day!"

Arty punched in the code to the security system, did his funny little dance and stuck out his tongue, and the steel door to the bunker swung open. The three friends made their way up the spiral stairs and out through the grass-covered trapdoor they'd entered earlier that day.

The first thing they noticed was the silence. Arty's street was eerily quiet, like a meditating mouse or a monk with a mouthful of cheese. The chaos of before was completely gone: There were no car noises in the streets, and even the birds in the sky seemed to have taken a break from their warbling.

"Whoa. It's like the inside of Great Aunt Doris's head," said Emmie. "Quiet and totally empty."

Sam and Arty couldn't bring themselves to laugh. They crossed the lawn and peered inside the window of Arty's house. There seemed to be someone inside, so they went in through the back door to take a look.

Arty gasped in horror at what he saw.

In the middle of the living room, his brother, Jesse, stood, staring at himself in the mirror. This, to be fair, was pretty normal for Jesse, who did rather like to look at his square jaw and to play around with his boy-band hair. But something was different.

That's actually an understatement. Let me revise: Something was more than different; something was catastrophically *wrong*. Jesse wasn't moving at all. In fact, his arms were stuck in midair like he was shaking maracas, and he had turned as gray as a wet Sunday,

and a cloud of smoke was slowly wafting up into the air around him.

Arty gave him a shove, but he was rooted to the spot. His skin was rough like stone, and there was no movement whatsoever in his body.

"Whoa . . . ," said Arty. "I mean, I always wanted to shut my brother up, but this . . ."

"I've never read about a disease like it," said Emmie. "This is next level!"

Sam, however, was convinced he knew what was going on. "You haven't read about a disease like it because it's not a disease," he insisted. "The Sailor's Sleep curse is real. And Sitting Duck is in trouble."

CHAPTER SIX

Arty and Emmie were alarmed. They weren't usually ones to believe in curses. They were all about science and reason and, you know, things that actually exist. Sam, too, was normally like that, but he was firmly convinced that the Sailor's Sleep curse was real. Arty and Emmie decided to give him the benefit of the doubt.

"We need to find out what we're dealing with, one way or another. So what now?" Emmie asked.

Sam nodded. Arty rubbed his chin, which was always a good sign. It meant that he was coming up with an idea. (Either that or he was scratching his invisible beard.) The more he rubbed, the better the idea. Eventually, his eyes lit up, as if a light bulb had appeared above his head.

"If Tweedy and his staff did move the treasure, then it would be at the museum, right?" Arty said. "We should go there and see what we find."

"That's true," Sam said. "And if the treasure is there, we take it back to the *Silver Mallard* and the curse will be lifted."

Emmie was skeptical, but it was the best (and only) idea they had. So, they left poor Jesse where he was standing, unable to move, and headed back out into Sitting Duck.

As they entered the town square, they found another eerie scene. It was as if the whole of Sitting Duck itself had been turned into a weird kind of museum. Old Mrs. Missus was out

Sitting Duck's Historical Curses

Sailor's Sleep wasn't the first instance of Sitting Duck being cursed, you won't be surprised to hear. In fact, this town has survived more scourges than you can imagine, which is why I will list them here for you. You're welcome.

- The Curse of the Witch's Tomb: When local witch and popular lass Hortensia Hardbottle died, she left a curse on her tomb. Any would-be grave robbers would do well to leave it alone, lest their legs turn to brooms and their noses turn into snakes!

- The Saddles of Doom: When legendary rodeo rider Bill Buckin' Buckley was thrown from his horse back in Sitting

Duck's Wild West years, he cursed the town as he lay dying. From then on, saddles caused sore butts. Even when you're riding a bike.

- Dunderson's Revenge: Unlucky Gus Dunderson, true to his name, was the most unfortunate fellow in all of Sitting Duck. While on one of his usually fruitless bird-watching expeditions, a duck fell on his head. The duck was fine, but Gus was not. With his final breath, he cursed the town of Sitting Duck to be as unlucky as he was. Which, now that I think about it, explains quite a lot.

walking her pet poodle, but the poodle was nowhere to be seen. Instead, Mrs. Missus just stood stock-still, leash in hand but nowhere to go.

Sam and Arty both hoped their parents were okay. Wherever they were, it couldn't be as bad as being stuck outside like a statue. Emmie was less bothered and even had a cheery smile on her face.

"Finally, no more Great Aunt Doris. She'll be as still as a statue right now," Emmie beamed. "Just think, no more toenail-cutting duties. No more tiptoeing out of the house, ducking under the alarm system, and dodging evil old Attila."

(Emmie's great aunt Doris had an unfortunate cat that rather enjoyed making Emmie's life a misery.) She smiled like a dog with his favorite bone. "What a time to be alive, eh?"

Sam and Arty just nodded, unconvinced, but happy for Emmie nonetheless. Still, something Emmie said made Sam think.

"If your great aunt Doris had ended up a statue, like all these people in this street, that means that no one is left in Sitting Duck. There are no adults, no more kids, no one to tell us what to do. . . ."

"And that means we're in charge!" Arty finished.

The children's eyes lit up. Okay, the apocalypse had pretty much come to pass, and there were no humans that could move a muscle in at least a ten-mile radius. But that didn't mean something good couldn't come out of it, right? Sam, Arty, and Emmie were just looking on the bright side. I, for one, would be happy for the world to end and finally prove my predictions of doom are true. I mean, why do you think I keep writing these tales?

"We wouldn't have to go to school," Sam gasped. "We could drive around in fancy cars . . . play baseball from dawn until sunset . . . eat junk food whenever we wanted. . . ."

Arty giggled and broke into a dance. He caught sight of Mrs. Jenkins's World of Candy down the street, doors wide open and no one looking after the place. His mouth watered at the thought of triple fudge delights and candy zombies. (With candy zombies, you get to eat *their* brains.)

Sam's eyes widened as he thought of being in charge of a whole town, all by himself. He spotted another statuesque resident of Sitting Duck down the road: Officer Hardnose. Hardnose had always stopped him playing ball in the park after that one time Sam had accidentally hit a home run that also smashed the blue and red lights on the

top of Hardnose's car. Turns out cops are really into those flashing lights and they don't appreciate them being destroyed. Sam now took his revenge the only way he knew how and pantsed the officer. He snickered at Officer Hardnose's boxers, which were covered with hearts.

"Nice work!" said Arty, who'd returned from Mrs. Jenkins's shop with a bagful of candy and a sugar-crazed twinkle in his eye. "That sure taught him!"

Sam nodded. It definitely had taught him. Although somehow it wasn't as fun when he couldn't see Hardnose's temper go through the roof. They had the town to themselves, but it didn't even feel like home.

There was a scream from behind them, and Arty and Sam turned in unison to see Emmie wide-eyed and trembling with fright. They rushed over to see what was wrong.

"It can't be," she said. "It can't be. . . ."

Sam and Arty followed her trembling finger, until they saw the familiar figure of Phoebe Bowles trundling up the street with Glitterpuff.

"H-h-how did *you* survive the apocalypse?" Emmie gasped.

Phoebe looked around her, without a care in the world.

"The what?" she asked.

"The end of the world, the Sailor's Sleep curse?"

Phoebe looked around her. "Oh . . . I thought things seemed a little quieter today than, like, usual."

Emmie cried out in exasperation, but Sam and Arty just giggled.

"I was at yoga," Phoebe continued. "Then I, like, went to the spa, for some pampering? Which to be honest, it looks like you could do with."

Emmie balled her fists in anger. "What. Are. You. Talking. About?" she said through gritted teeth.

"See for yourself," Phoebe said, holding up a small compact mirror.

Emmie peered into it and let out a little gasp. Right on the end of her nose was a tiny green spot, which was just beginning to grow. . . .

CHAPTER SEVEN

Emmie laughed and looked nervously around at the others.

"It's n-not the curse," she said, unsure of herself for once. "It's just a zit, you know. A friendly green zit. I get them all the time. They're green because, erm, I eat a lot of spinach . . . ?"

Sam raised an eyebrow—he wasn't so sure. In fact, he was downright worried for one of his best friends. To be honest, I'd be pretty worried, too. That green spot looked a lot like something you'd get if you had the Sailor's Sleep curse. But then again, I also don't want to disagree with Emmie, because she'll beat me up or something. If she says she's fine, she's fine . . . right?

"But you hate spinach," Arty said.

Sam just nudged him in the ribs. "Shussh, you idiot!"

Arty got the message and decided to keep quiet, but he wasn't happy about it. Emmie fidgeted nervously, like a badger in a beehive.

"Or it's just a cold," she said. "Yeah, that'll be it."

Sam nodded, but deep down he knew Emmie was ill. He had to find a way to reverse the curse before it was too late.

"Well, whatever it is, let's not stand around yakking about it. We've got a world to save!" he said. The others agreed, and together, they set off through their apocalyptic town full of statuesque people to the grand old Sitting Duck Museum, in the hopes of finding the treasure

Caruthers had stolen from Merfolk Island.

The giant, old building was right in the center of Sitting Duck, just by the Town Hall, and housed everything of interest in Sitting Duck. It even had a wing devoted to the zombie hordes and alien invasions of recent years. Frankly, I'd want to forget things like that, but no, not the eccentric museum curator, Mr. Tweedy.

As they made their way there, an eerie silence haunted them. Emergency vehicles still lined the streets, and a thin drizzle of rain came down, dampening the people turned to living statues by the curse. Finally, they arrived at the museum and made their way up the wide stone stairs, passing tourists and visitors turned to statues, and pushed open the museum doors.

They entered a large atrium and looked around eagerly, but, not too surprisingly, the treasure wasn't there. That's because no one would be dumb enough to leave a ton of gold lying around, not even Mr. Tweedy.

"So, like, where do we start?" Phoebe asked.

Arty looked around. "Over here, see," he said. He pointed toward a large banner advertising the Armitage Caruthers exhibition. "Meet coin collector extraordinaire and owner of Albertus the Duck, the mighty Armitage Caruthers!" Frankly, I find the sign to be an odd choice. Why not mention the many merfolk he vanquished, the treasure he plundered, or, you know, the town he founded?

"Like, duh," Phoebe said. "That totally makes sense."

"Let's go," said Sam.

Emmie started coughing, and her three friends shot nervous glances her way.

The kids dodged the ticket collector, who was now still as stone, and ducked under the barrier. As they entered the exhibit, Sam marveled at all the cool artifacts from his hero. This was more like it! One of the walls was lined with portraits of Caruthers and his exploits. In one painting, he was wrestling a giant octopus; in another, he was swimming with dolphins; in a third, he was chatting to his pet duck, Albertus, way up in the crow's nest of the *Silver Mallard*. Sam oohed and aahed. Caruthers's exploits were a joy to behold.

"Wow!" Sam gasped. "I wish that was me sailing the high seas."

He checked out another room, where Caruthers's portrait stood alongside that of his

ancestors. The captain sat proudly, chest puffed
out, smirking mischievously for the world to see.
Sam noticed that he had one green eye and one
brown eye.

Next to Caruthers were
thirty or so other
portraits, all of his
descendants.

"Cool," he gasped.
"Maybe I'm descended
from Caruthers, too!"

"I think your dad would have mentioned it," Arty laughed, scanning his eyes across the pictures. As he peered closer, he noticed something weird about Caruthers and his heirs. The early Caruthers ancestors all had little plaques under each painting claiming that they were mayors or bigwigs or other fancy, rich people, and they wore colorful silk clothes and carried impressive weapons. But over time, the people in the portraits looked less successful. One of them had a mouthful of rotten teeth. Another had a ripped hat and a wooden sword. Eventually, the records stopped about fifty years ago, and then there were no more portraits at all.

"Aw," said Sam as they reached the end of the gallery. "Maybe I am descended from him, and it just got lost in time."

"But probably not," Arty said. "I mean, you do have all your teeth!"

Emmie let out a whistle like a frightened bird, which according to their secret whistling signal meant *Come here, now!*

Arty and Sam came running over. Emmie and Phoebe stood outside a door with a sign that read RESTRICTED AREA. Like any good action hero and world-saver, she didn't let a little thing like a sign put her off.

"C'mon, guys," she said, in between a cough and a sneeze. "If the treasure's anywhere, it'll be in here."

Sam couldn't help but notice another little green spot had appeared on her forehead. His brow wrinkled with concern, but Emmie pushed open the heavy wooden door before he could say anything, and they all dived inside.

"For the love of history!" Arty cried. "Still nothing."

The kids sighed; once again, there was no treasure to be found. However, they were obviously somewhere *official* and *important*, and it didn't take long before they *did* find something of interest. There were glass cabinets with the doors flung open, artifacts strewn about the place, and on a huge wooden desk, dusty old parchments lay piled up just waiting to be rummaged through.

"Maybe there are some clues here," Arty said. "There's all sorts of stuff. . . ."

He picked up the nearest parchment and whistled. "Whoa . . . I think we've hit the jackpot. This is from Armitage Caruthers himself. . . . It must be part of his captain's log!"

Sam's eyes nearly popped out of their sockets. "Lemme see! Lemme see!" he gasped.

Sure enough, when Arty handed it over, Sam could see that it was an ancient parchment. It was crinkly and brown, as if the paper were about to give way any second. It smelled like the inside of a musty old sock drawer, but that didn't matter because he distinctly saw the signature of Armitage Caruthers himself, scrawled in ink along the bottom.

"Quick, what does it say?" Emmie asked.

Sam cleared his throat. "It says . . ."

Captain's Log:

Day 20.

Hello there, log, just me again. How's your bark? Ha! We do have such jokes. Obviously you don't have bark. You're a diary log, not a <u>log</u> log.

Anywho, I thought I'd update you on some very important developments. Firstly, my big toe seems to have grown by ¾ of an inch. It's a miracle. I've always wanted a large toe and now the day has finally arrived!

Secondly, I had a rather delicious dinner of dried goat and stewed limes. My crewmates turned their noses up at it. But you know me, if it's got hooves and fruit in it, I'll eat it.

Thirdly, but of much less importance, there seems to be a curse going around the ship. At first, I thought they were just doing the good old pirate jig, but then the blighters stopped moving and wouldn't do any work . . .

The parchment was cut off midsentence, but the kids looked at one another in alarm.

"He sounds, like, crazy," Phoebe said. Glitterpuff yapped in approval.

"He sounds like fun," Sam said.

"He sounds like he knew all about the Sailor's Sleep curse," said Arty.

Emmie coughed and spluttered. She was about to reach for the scroll herself, but her body was convulsed. It looked like she was doing the old pirate jig Caruthers mentioned.

Finally, she admitted it. "And it looks like I have it, too!"

CHAPTER EIGHT

Emmie let out a little wail and then balled her fists in defiance. Sam and Arty each placed a hand on one of her shoulders. Even Phoebe looked downhearted. Time was running out for Emmie. They had to figure out a way to reverse the curse.

"We'll fix this," Sam said.

"No doubt," Arty confirmed.

"If we, like, have to," Phoebe chimed in.

Emmie smiled. If they fought this thing together, she knew they'd beat it. Either that or she'd be spending the rest of her life as a statue, probably getting pooped on by pigeons.

Suddenly, Glitterpuff let out a shrill *yip*, and

the door to the office slammed shut. The kids watched in horror at the two giant men looming over them. Both of them looked like barrels with legs or rhinoceroses with human faces or hot-air balloons with muscles. . . . (You get the idea— they were *big*.) One had a square chin as hard as a hammer. The other had a steely glint in his eyes that said he meant business. And by business, he meant the business of punching.

"Fellow survivors!" Sam beamed. "We were hoping we weren't the only ones. . . ."

"Sam, I don't think—" Arty began. But before he could finish, the two men puffed out their chests and each took a step closer to them, their towering forms casting shadows across the kids' faces.

"Shut it, you worms," said one.

"Yeah. What he said," said the other.

The kids looked at one another in fear.

Arty whispered to Sam: "They're Slim and Slimmer. They're guards at the museum."

Sam wondered how Arty knew this, but then he remembered his best friend was a huge nerd and liked nothing more than to spend time at museums and libraries. He also wondered how two giant dudes like these guys ended up with names like Slim and Slimmer, and realized it must be a joke. These guys were built like sacks of potatoes.

"What are you lot doing here?" Slim asked, making a fist.

"Erm, we're just admiring the plants," Emmie said, pointing to a large begonia that stood in the corner of the room. "Isn't it lo-ve-ly!" she said in

a singsong voice that was about the most unusual thing Sam had witnessed all day.

Phoebe played along. "It's simply de-vine! What a miracle of nature . . ."

Sadly, Slim's and Slimmer's large muscles didn't extend to them also having big brains. They whispered among themselves, wondering what to do with the children. Sam heard them say things like "but the boss didn't say anything about survivors . . ." and "maybe we should just bonk them over the head and have done with it," at which point Sam decided they had to get out of there.

Sam gave a low whistle. Emmie and Arty nodded. Phoebe didn't know what the whistle meant, but she nodded along anyway just 'cause she didn't want to feel left out.

While Slim and Slimmer bickered like old ladies about what to do with them, Sam, Arty, Emmie, and Phoebe edged their way around the corner of the room. They tiptoed like cat burglars burgling a whole cattery of cats and made it to the door. Sam twisted the knob, and they silently crept out. . . .

Glitterpuff let out a *yap*.

"Wait a minute!" said Slimmer, who unfortunately spoke Tiny Dog. "Get back here, you slimy toads!"

The kids made a run for it, sprinting across the shiny wooden floor of the museum. Their legs pumped and their arms flailed and they almost would've made it if it weren't for Armitage Caruthers. Sam, speedy as he was, couldn't avoid the giant stone statue in the center of the room.

Before he knew it, he'd bashed right into it and fell sprawling on the floor. The others turned to help him up, but by then it was too late. They were completely cornered.

"Gotcha, you slippery eels!" said Slim, grinning wickedly.

Sam rubbed his sore head and opened his

eyes. For a moment, he was pleased as he saw the familiar shapes of Arty, Emmie, and Phoebe come into focus around him. But then his heart sank as he realized he had no idea where he was.

"What the—?" he began, scrabbling to his feet. "Where are we?"

"We have no idea," said Emmie, who by now was covered in green spots. "They blindfolded us and said they were holding us here for 'safekeeping.'"

Sam looked around. The walls were wooden, with no windows, and at one end of the room was a giant metal prison door. He let out a whistle.

"We're in a pickle this time," he said.

"Yeah, no kidding," Arty agreed.

Phoebe scolded them both. "I knew I, like,

should've gone to my dance class instead of hanging out with you guys."

Emmie grumbled. She was struggling with the Sailor's Sleep curse, and her body was starting to turn stiff and gray, but she still managed to take a swipe at Phoebe. "Well, then maybe you should have," she spat. "Your stupid little rat dog got us caught and nearly did Sam in altogether."

"Hey!" Phoebe said. "He's not a rat dog. He's a precious wittle wovey dovey cute fluffy wuffy . . ."

Phoebe continued in this way for some time, so the others put their minds to work figuring out where they were.

Arty pointed out something disturbing he'd found in the corner of the room while Sam had been out for the count.

"Looks like this guy didn't make it out alive,"

Arty said. He pointed at a grisly skeleton in the corner of the room. His clothes hung off what was left of him like rags, his jaunty hat just barely hanging on to his skull.

"Yikes," said Emmie. "Poor guy."

Sam looked closer and rummaged around in the skeleton's shirt pocket.

"Hey, look," he said. "There's a letter. . . ."

He pulled out an aged piece of paper.

"*Dearest Jennifer . . . I am in prison now, but I will be out of here before thy knowst it,*" Sam read.

"Yeah, good luck with that, pal," said Emmie.

"Shhh," said Sam. "Look at this. It's signed by someone called Boatswain Rogers."

Suddenly, a heaving motion flung Sam off his feet. He barreled right into the skeleton, sending the bones scattering around the cell. Then the room seemed to crash down again, pinning the children to the floor.

"What in the name of science?" Arty asked as he was flung about the place like a penny stuck in a washing machine.

But deep down Arty knew what was in the name of science. After surviving five disasters, he was becoming almost fluent in catastrophe. He put two and two together. Luckily, this time he came up with four.

"First, the weird wooden cell, then the letter from the boatswain, and now we're bobbing up and down like kittens in a puddle," he cried. "It can only mean one thing. . . ." Then he paused, to add a bit of drama . . . Then a bit more . . . Then finally . . .

"We're on board the *Silver Mallard*! And it's setting sail!"

CHAPTER NINE

Sam's eyes nearly popped out of his head. He couldn't believe that he was on the very same ship as Armitage Caruthers, about to sail the high seas. Or, the sea just off Sitting Duck. Or, at the very least, the Leaky Tap River.

"This is awesome," he gasped. "I haven't been this excited since at least last Tuesday." Sam thought back to last Tuesday. Ah, what a day. Grilled cheese for lunch and a walk in the park with his dad. When Sam's not an all-out action hero, he likes the simpler things in life. Which made him think, *Maybe I should really get on with the business of getting out of here and saving my parents and one of my best friends.*

"This is so *not* awesome," Arty protested. "We don't even know where we're going!"

"And who on Earth is steering this thing?" Emmie asked. "Slim and Slimmer?"

Sam didn't have the answers to all these questions, but he was sure as sugar that he was going to find out.

"Well, let's get out of this place, then," he said. "Quick, Arty, do you still have your Swiss Barmy Knife? We could really use a skeleton key right about now."

Arty rummaged around in his pocket and pulled out the knife. He flicked through the attachments— colored pencil, magnifying glass, banana—until he eventually alighted on just what he was after.

"That's funny," Arty said, "because I have a skeleton key right here!"

Arty put the key in the lock and jiggled it around a bit. The creaking, old iron gate screeched like a cat in a tornado, but it was no use. No matter how much he tried, the lock wouldn't turn. He tried to wrench it one more time, but the key snapped, and he had to fish the remains of it out of the lock.

"Oh man!" he cried. "What are we going to do now?"

The kids bobbed up and down as the *Silver Mallard* sailed to who-knows-where. They all looked green around the gills, apart from Emmie, who was turning an alarming shade of gray as the Sailor's Sleep took hold.

"I have an idea," said Phoebe.

Sam, Arty, and Emmie turned to her in surprise. Phoebe Bowles didn't have ideas. Phoebe Bowles usually had complaints or pink glittery hair bands. Phoebe Bowles drank fancy juice and did yoga, and she didn't notice when apocalypses struck her town. Her favorite juice drink was orange, strangeberry, and banana fizz. Her favorite yoga pose was the Flying Ballerina.

But this time, Phoebe was going to prove them all wrong.

"Like, look there," she said, pointing to a spot on the other side of the cell door. In the corner, another poor sailor lay all skeletal and gross and like he could do with a good meal pretty soonish.

"So?" Emmie asked.

"So, look closer. . . . Can you see that shiny thing? I think it might be a key."

Sure enough, by what used to be the sailor's hip, a bright piece of metal sparkled in the gloom.

"You're right!" Arty cried. "That guy must have been the jailer."

"But how do we get it?" Emmie huffed, sticking her arm through one of the metal bars. "It's too far away."

Phoebe looked glum and rubbed her chin for a second.

Beside her, Glitterpuff yapped.

Then Glitterpuff barked.

And then Glitterpuff got on to his back legs and did a small dance that looked a lot like the tango.

Eventually, Phoebe noticed.

"That's it," she cried. "We can use Glitterpuff to squeeze through the bars and grab the keys!"

"Good thinking, Phoebe," Sam said. "Let's try it."

Phoebe placed Glitterpuff at the jail door and ushered him through the metal bars. Once he'd wriggled his surprisingly large butt through, he immediately ran over to the skeletal sailor and began chewing on what used to be his leg.

"No!" Phoebe whined. "Very naughty boy, Puffy. Go for the key. The key!"

Phoebe thought that maybe if she spoke louder, Glitterpuff would eventually understand her. It didn't quite work, but there was something

in the tone of her
voice that must have
done the trick because "Puffy" soon
snaffled up the key and brought it back through
the bars.

"You did it!" she cried, bundling him up into
her arms. The dog seemed to smile and settled
back down into Phoebe's handbag. Even Emmie
patted him on the head for doing such a good job.

"Nice one, Glitterpuff," said Sam. He plucked the key from the ground, wiped off the doggy spit on the back of his sleeves, and thrust the key in the lock. There was a grinding sound and the iron bars rattled, but soon the door swung open and they were free.

"Woo-hoo!" Arty yelled. "Now let's get out of here."

"Hey, wait up," Emmie called. The effects of the curse were slowing her down. She was fighting hard, but she was already becoming a living statue. Sam and Phoebe took ahold of one arm each and helped her move around the hull of the boat. Arty looked on, nervously.

"We've got ya!" Sam cried.

"Urgh, you're like a one-ton weight," Phoebe huffed.

"Hey!" said Emmie, "I *am* turning to stone if you hadn't noticed."

Arty led the way through the warren of corridors at the bottom of the boat. It was almost completely dark. The only light there came in through broken wooden slats and eerie, flickering gas lamps.

"This way," he said. "I think. . . ."

He led them up the narrow stairs. They hadn't made it to the top, but they were obviously in another level of the ship. Arty took one of the lamps from the wall and looked around. The whole area was covered in huge wooden crates, all piled up on top of one another.

"Hey," he said, "maybe we can find some treasure."

"Well, make it quick," said Sam. "We need to know where we're going."

Arty cracked open one of the boxes. He peered inside and shone his lamp into the gloom. He let out a sigh when he found the treasure wasn't there.

"Nothing," he sighed. "Just a load of old bottles."

Sam peered over and took a look. "That's weird . . . ," he said.

The bottles were ancient; it looked as if they had been there with the original crew hundreds of years ago. The labels on the front were torn and peeling, but Sam could still make out what they said.

"Grog," he whispered. "Just what they served at the Founder's Day celebration."

Painted onto the side of the box was a giant skull and crossbones, in blood red. Arty lifted the lamp and shone it around the room. All the crates had the same skull-and-crossbones sign on them. It looked like a warning.

"But that would mean—" Sam began, but he didn't get a chance to finish.

There was a scuffle from behind, and a loud thudding on the ship's steps. Before they had a chance to hide, two familiar, burly figures were standing right in front of them. Phoebe gasped in fright.

"Well, well, well," said Slim. "The little maggots tried to escape, did they? The boss is not going to like that, is he now?"

"No, siree," said Slimmer. "The boss is not going to like that at all."

CHAPTER TEN

Sam, Arty, Emmie, and Phoebe were ushered onto the top deck, Slim and Slimmer roughly shoving them from behind. As they emerged into the light, Sam shielded his eyes. He'd grown used to the dim surroundings of the cell. Now, in front of him, he saw the impressive white sails of the *Silver Mallard* billowing in the breeze, and the bright sunshine bouncing off the wet deck. He was desperate to explore the ship and make a dash for it, but he was pulled back by Slim, who wasn't going to let him go anywhere.

"Not so fast, wriggler," Slim growled.

Despite the fact that Sam was in the custody of a giant henchman who was most certainly up to no good, he couldn't believe he was on board the amazing ship. The others seemed less thrilled, I have to tell you. But at least they'd noticed something Sam hadn't, while he'd been ogling the masts and sails.

Arty cocked his head and directed Sam's vision toward something amazing. Amid the piles of ropes on deck, there were big boxes overflowing with treasure.

"Whoa!" he gasped. "Check it out."

Gold coins were strewn across the floor. Emerald-encrusted swords lay piled up in the corner like unwanted brooms, next to a heap of diamond-encrusted scepters. There must have been millions of dollars' worth of loot. Sam, though, was puzzled. If the treasure hadn't been moved off the ship, then why had Sitting Duck come down

with the curse?

"It's awesome!" said Arty.

"It's so shiny," Phoebe added.

"Yes," said another, lower voice. "It's

quite something, isn't it?"

The kids turned to see the figure

of Mr. Tweedy, the museum curator,

towering over them.

He had one hand on the steering wheel and the other on his hip, like he was the proud owner of the vessel. He had a wide grin on his face like a happy dog that'd just been given his favorite bone, and his eyes twinkled in the sunlight. But the way he spoke sounded like a snake that had just caught sight of his favorite food and was getting ready to strike.

"You?" Sam asked, surprised. "I don't understand—"

Sam had never considered Mr. Tweedy to be some kind of bad guy. Yes, a total history nerd to rival Arty at his most uncool, but a bad guy? No. He had a nice suit and a jazzy bow tie and curly hair that bounced in the breeze like a rubber band, and if history has taught us anything, it is that people in bow ties with ridiculous hair are fine. Right?

As it turns out, wrong.

As Sam looked closer at Mr. Tweedy, he could see that he had one green eye and one brown eye. Something jogged his memory. In fact, it was less a jog and more like a sprint. Tweedy's eyes were just like the ones in the painting of Armitage Caruthers and his descendants. It was a pretty unusual thing to have, and he couldn't remember having even seen it real life. He couldn't help but wonder:

"Your eyes," he said. "They're just like—"

Tweedy's face darkened, and his cheery demeanor disappeared in a flash. A frown creased his brow, and he puffed out his chest in defiance. His hands gripped the ship's wheel tighter as it bobbed up and down on the waters.

"That's correct," he said icily. "Indeed, I am descended from none other than Armitage

Caruthers himself—"

"Awesome!" Sam cried, apparently still unaware of the danger they were in.

"Shut it!" said Slim, tightening his grip on Sam's arm. Sam looked warily around at Arty, Phoebe, and Emmie. Emmie was looking grayer by the minute.

"Yes," said Mr. Tweedy. "'Shut it,' indeed. It's my turn to talk, and I expect you fools to listen."

The kids snapped to attention.

"Caruthers was my ancestor, yes, but the fact is not 'awesome' as you so hastily said, young sir. On the contrary, Caruthers is a bane on my life and yours. The man was a pirate, a blaggard, and a fool. He founded this town that we see before us, but it has been the scene of nothing but endless catastrophe. From the Great Octopus Invasion

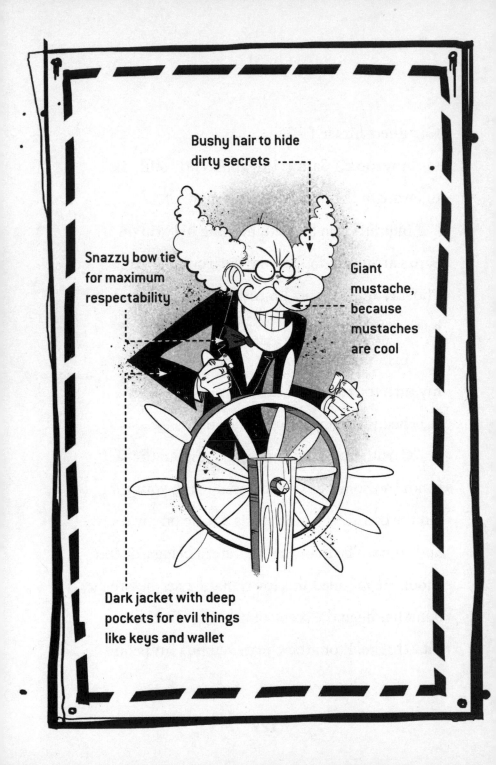

to the recent undead apocalypse, Sitting Duck is nothing but a magnet for trouble."

"He does have a point there," said Arty. "Things have been a bit disastrous."

Even Slim and Slimmer grunted in agreement.

"The curse!" Sam blurted. "Sitting Duck is cursed, though, right?"

Mr. Tweedy cackled like a maniac. He clutched his armpits and guffawed like an octopus was tickling him. Sam was guessing that was a no.

"What fools you are!" Tweedy laughed. "You should know that there's no such thing as a curse, my friends. After all Sitting Duck has been through, it's not magic and superstition you should be worried about, but regular people!"

(And aliens.)

"That mad professor created the zombies,"

Tweedy continued. "The astronomer brought us the aliens. Dr. Goode brainwashed everyone, and one of you created an evil robot! Not to mention the girl that unleashed giant spiders upon us."

"But the illness," said Arty. "What causes the illness?"

At this, a smile swept across Tweedy's face. He pointed down to a wooden crate, full of empty bottles of grog. "It's simple really. . . . A three-hundred-and-fifty-year-old dose of infected grog. That seemed to do the trick quite nicely. Your precious curse is nothing more than an old pirate bacteria! Just a drop of revenge against the idiots in this town who allow themselves to be overrun."

If Sam were in full control of his arms, he would have smacked himself in the forehead. *Of course*, he thought. *Nearly everyone drank the grog*

at the Founder's Day celebration . . . even Emmie,
until she spat it out . . .

"But anyway, enough talk," Mr. Tweedy said
darkly. "It's time to do something about Sitting
Duck once and for all. With the town's people out
of working order, I'm going to put a stop to this
nonsense for good. Soon, Sitting Duck shall be no
more."

"How, you miserable old trout?" Emmie asked
through stony lips. "Are you going to 'sail' it into
oblivion?"

"Funnily enough, yes!" he said. "It probably
escaped your notice, but this ship is actually
packed with dynamite. And I'm planning on
using it. You see, right now, we're on the Leaky
Tap River, heading north. And do you know what
happens when we go farther north?"

Sam did not know what would happen, but he was hoping it was something nice.

"We reach the Sitting Duck Dam," Tweedy said proudly. "A modern marvel. Something Sitting Duck can truly be proud of."

Sam didn't like where this was going.

"Which makes it such a shame that I'm going to blow it to smithereens," he said gleefully, his bow tie practically twirling around as he said it.

"You can't!" Sam gasped. "Sitting Duck will be destroyed."

"Yes, young sir," Tweedy continued. "That is rather the point. The dam will be destroyed, Lake Deep Puddle will be unleashed, and Sitting Duck will be wiped off the map for good. Neat, huh? My rotten ancestor created this mess, but I'm going to finish it."

Sam, Arty, Emmie, and Phoebe struggled against the tight hold of Slim and Slimmer, but it was to no avail.

"Oh, calm down," said Tweedy. "I would relax if I were you. It's not like you'll be affected."

"What do you mean?" Sam asked slowly.

"Oh, didn't I mention it?" Tweedy said. "You'll be long gone by the time the dam is blown up."

He let out a cackle, and his suit ruffled in the strong breeze.

"Guards!" he bellowed. "It's time for our guests to walk the plank!"

CHAPTER ELEVEN

The kids twisted and struggled as hard as they could, but there was no escaping Slim and Slimmer. Mr. Tweedy cackled.

"Don't worry, children. I'm sure it will be quick!" he snorted. "Ah—I see I have one less of you to worry about anyway."

Sam looked over to where Tweedy was pointing. Emmie was as still as a stone. Even her wild hair was gray and unmoving, and her smiley face—okay, she wasn't that smiley—was frozen.

"NO!" Sam and Arty yelled. But it was no use. Emmie was totally unmoving, and there was nothing they could do. Sam balled his fists in anger and kicked against the muscle mountain that was Slim, striking Slim's shin, but that only made the brute angrier.

Slim and Slimmer hauled the children into the air and deposited them at the edge of the ship.

"Serves you right, you slimy critters," Slim said.

"Yeah," Slimmer agreed. "Let's see if you can swim, eh?"

Sam, Arty, and Phoebe looked at one another fearfully. There was nowhere left to go.

"Go on, then," Mr. Tweedy coaxed. "Off you go. See you later. *Au revoir, auf Wiedersehen,* tatty-bye, and good luck . . ."

With Slim and Slimmer standing in front of them, arms crossed and muscles bulging, Sam, Arty, and Phoebe had no other choice. They climbed up onto the side of the ship and onto the plank. Gingerly, they made their way toward the edge and looked down in horror at the churning water below.

"This is not good. This is so not good," said Arty, in a statement of the blindingly obvious, as the river water splashed up at him.

"Erm, guys, I really don't want to get my dress wet," said Phoebe. "You see, it's designer, and it's, like, kind of expensive and—"

"Erm, Phoebe, that's nice, but we kind of have other things to worry about right now, in case you didn't notice," said Sam.

Phoebe just fluffed her hair and rolled her eyes.

"Get on with it!" shouted Tweedy from the boat. "We haven't got all day."

Sam readied himself. This really was the end. After the zombies and aliens and giant spiders, he had thought he could beat whatever Sitting Duck threw at him. But apparently not. He was trumped by a maniac museum man with a grudge against his dead ancestor the size of the Great Octopus Invasion. It's always the ones you least expect!

"Okay, guys, get ready," Sam said. "Three, two—"

Suddenly, something caught his eye.

Something shiny and metal and pointy and sharp,

and something that was about to save their day.
Emmie wasn't *completely* statuefied yet; she'd
fooled them all. She winked at Sam and grabbed
something from the treasure trove next to her.
With her final ounce of strength, just before
she turned entirely to stone with a poof of gray
smoke, she flung the metal object through the air.

Sam leaped in the air and snatched the
sword from the sky. Luckily, he got the handle
and not the pointy end—that would have been
unfortunate and not at all as planned.

Tweedy growled in anger and alarm. "Finish
them!" he yelled.

Slim and Slimmer barreled their way onto
the plank. The whole thing shook up and down,
threatening to send all five of them into the water.

"I think I'm gonna barf," said Arty.

"Ew!" said Phoebe. "If he throws up, then I'm going to throw up, and that's not cool."

Slim and Slimmer moved forward. The plank shook wildly, sending Arty and Phoebe over the side.

"No!" Sam shouted in horror, but to his surprise, his friends had both managed to grab on to the side of the boat. They were safe.

As they scrambled onto the deck, Arty shouted back to him. "You've got this, Sam!"

Sam held on to the sword handle tightly. The handle was made of gold, encrusted with bright green emeralds and dark rubies, and it curved around Sam's hand. The blade was rounded and flat, and it shone like the day it was forged.

"Come get us," Sam growled.

They were so big that they seemed to take up

the whole of Sam's vision. With their big hands
like plates of ham, they lunged forward and tried
to grab him.

But Sam was too quick for them—he's escaped
many a disaster before, after all. He lunged back
at them with the sword, scaring them silly. Then,
seizing his chance, he swiped at Slim's ankles with
the flat of the blade, and Slim went tumbling
into the water.

"Arghhh!" he yelled as he splashed into the Leaky Tap River.

Slimmer roared forward with the fury of an antelope with a migraine. I don't know if you have ever had the misfortune of facing an antelope under these conditions, but it is truly a terrifying sight to behold. It's no surprise then that Sam had even less trouble dispatching him. Sam landed a blow right on Slimmer's hips, which sent him tumbling into the water, alongside his brawny colleague.

"Good work," Arty cried.

Sam beamed. "I told you I belong on the high seas fighting bad guys!"

Sam inched along the wooden plank and back onto the ship. Mr. Tweedy roared with rage and yanked on the steering wheel. The ship lurched to the left, sending the kids crashing to the deck, and the cool pirate sword went flying from Sam's hand and straight over the edge.

"Darn it!" he yelled.

Tweedy roared with delight. "Now what are you going to do, you little bandit? Nothing, that's what, because it's too late for you all."

As the ship veered, the kids couldn't help but notice the huge concrete dam coming into sight. It arched upward like a colossus, practically blocking out the sunlight. It kept the huge Lake Deep Puddle at bay, but Sam feared that it wouldn't be around for long, and soon the water would rush over Sitting Duck, destroying it for good.

"He's a maniac!" Sam yelled.

"The tidal wave alone will wash Sitting Duck out to sea," Arty gasped.

Tweedy laughed. "It seems I was wrong,

children. You *will* be around to see the end of Sitting Duck after all. It must bring a tear to the eye, eh? Considering the monsters and villains you lot have fought to get this far. But it's no use; new threats will always be around to take Sitting Duck down. It's just easier this way. I've already had my revenge on the residents; now it's time to eliminate the town itself."

"No," cried Sam. "We won't let you do this!"

Sam clambered up onto the main deck, where Tweedy stood manning the steering wheel. He tried to yank it in the other direction, but Tweedy had other ideas. He gave Sam an almighty shove, which sent him flying backward, and continued on his course.

"Nice try, little one," he cackled. "But just not good enough."

Tweedy brought a match out of his pocket and

scratched it against his corduroy trousers. The little flame burst into life. He carefully lit a fuse, which led all the way to the dynamite that was bundled up on deck and throughout the ship.

"And now," he declared, "time for some fireworks!"

CHAPTER TWELVE

Sam looked around frantically for something he could do, but he was fresh out of ideas. It was like his brain had gone into early hibernation for the winter. Very early, in fact, as it was summer.

"Arty, Phoebe," he said, "if we don't do something quick, Sitting Duck is going to be the next lost city of Atlantis!"

Sam and Arty looked at each other in alarm as the ship sailed toward doom. They'd never let Sitting Duck down at its time of need before, and if they couldn't get Tweedy off that wheel, they'd never get a chance again. Because they'd all be washed out to sea, living with the know-it-all dolphins and the smelly tuna and, worse, the evil merfolk.

"Erm, yoo-hoo," Phoebe piped up. "I think I, like, have an idea?"

Sam and Arty pricked up their ears. It wasn't normal for Phoebe Bowles to have one idea. So to have two ideas in one day was very unusual indeed.

"Just a little something I learned at the dog show," she explained. Phoebe let Glitterpuff down from her handbag and whispered something in his ear. Whatever she said had an almost hypnotic effect. Glitterpuff twirled around a few times like a dizzy ballerina, yipping cheerfully. But then he landed on all fours, growled, and took a long hard look at Tweedy.

"Go get him, Puffy Wuffy!" Phoebe yelled.

The Chihuahua motored across the ship like a tiny, furry remote-controlled car. He ran up to the main deck, where Tweedy was manning the steering wheel and, with a howl, clamped his teeth onto the villain's ankle and sunk them in deep.

"Yarrgh!" Tweedy yelled. "What in the name of holy moly? Get this monstrous beast off me!"

Tweedy had to lift his hands off the steering wheel in an attempt to bat the dog away. He flailed

about on the top deck, but Glitterpuff held strong.
Soon, Tweedy decided that it made sense to make
a run for it—he couldn't stand the yapping little
critter anymore. As Tweedy made a dash for it,
Glitterpuff let go and chased him around the
deck, yipping madly.

Eventually, Glitterpuff trapped Tweedy up
against a mast; his eyes were darting madly for
an escape route. There was nowhere left to run.
With one last look at the dog's tiny but powerful
chompers, Tweedy turned and climbed up the
central mast for dear life.

"Yeah!" Arty yelled. "Good dog!"

Phoebe smiled proudly. "He can be kind of
ferocious when he wants to be!"

Glitterpuff did a little victory dance and
cocked his leg for a celebratory wee on the mast.

Tweedy leered down from the crow's nest, way up high. "You might be smiling now, you beastly children, but you won't be in a minute!"

Sam looked up. Sure enough, the ship was still on a collision course with the dam, and the explosive fuse was shining bright. Any second now, it was about to blow.

"C'mon," Sam yelled to Arty. "Help me steer this thing."

Sam and Arty ran up onto the top deck and yanked on the wheel. Together, they pulled hard to the port side. For a minute, Sam had visions of sailing the high seas and fighting off pirates and sea monsters and man-eating octopuses. He would ride the waves and face down fierce storms, weather the craziest weather, and discover new lands and exciting mythical—

"Sam!" Arty yelled. "Quit daydreaming!"

Sam shook off the fantasy and yanked even harder on the steering wheel until it twirled in front of him. At last, the ship began to creak and turn. Its vast wooden bulk heaved up and down, and the water churned beneath it as the Leaky Tap River's current helped the ship turn ninety degrees to safety. Arty held on to statue-Emmie so she wouldn't roll across the deck.

"Phoebe!" Sam yelled. "Man the sails!"

Phoebe rushed to the other side of the deck to yank the sails into position. With the ship out of danger from smashing into the dam, they went full speed ahead and powered the ship back down the Leaky Tap River and into the harbor as fast as they could.

However, Arty, because he was clever like

that, decided he simply had to point out a small problem that everyone else had seemed to have forgotten about.

"Sam, buddy," he said. "There is still about a ton of explosives on board the ship, which are, erm, currently about to explode. Do you think maybe we should get off of this ship right this instant?"

"I'd say that is a pretty fine idea, Arty," Sam said. "A pretty fine idea indeed."

Together they raced back down the deck and hollered at Phoebe to "abandon ship!" She yelped in panic and grabbed Glitterpuff and stuffed him into her bag. The trusty dog quit his yapping and got ready for a nice bath in the chilly depths of the river.

"What about Emmie?" Arty asked frantically.

Sam racked his brain and suddenly it woke from early hibernation. He was not only going to save Emmie; Emmie was also going to save him. He grabbed his best pal and, together with Sam and Phoebe, prepared to jump.

"Farewell, farewell!" Tweedy intoned, from atop the mast. "Parting is such sweet sorrow. . . ."

"It is for you, pal," said Sam.

With an almighty leap, just like in a pretty darn cool action movie, Sam, Arty, and Phoebe jumped off the ship. A gigantic *BANG* erupted behind them and the explosives burst into life. Sam, Arty, Phoebe, and statue-Emmie were flung high into the air as the *Silver Mallard* exploded into oblivion.

The sky burned with fiery orange, and Sam felt the hairs on the back of his neck singe as the powerful explosives ripped across the sky.

Before they knew it, the four friends were splash landing in the Leaky Tap River. As they came up for air, Sam saw plumes of smoke billowing out behind them and wooden debris littering the surface of the water. He took a mental photograph as the once-proud *Silver Mallard* disappeared under the water, gurgling and groaning as it went. Mr. Tweedy was nowhere to be seen. A scoundrel all the way, but at least he went down with the ship.

"Blurgh!" Phoebe cried, coughing up a mouthful of water.

Glitterpuff yapped and doggy paddled to keep afloat. His execution was flawless because he *was* a dog. You're not about to see him do the butterfly stroke. That's almost exclusively for butterflies.

Arty struggled in the water, flapping his arms around like a windmill in a hurricane.

"Argh," he yelled. "Gimme a hand. . . ."

"Here," said Sam, who noticed his friend struggling. "Grab on."

Sam had turned Emmie over so she was on her back, her stone face pointing toward the sky. Arty and Emmie paddled over to join Sam. Glitterpuff climbed onto Emmie and curled up on her belly. The three friends held on tight to Emmie as they kicked their legs and slowly headed for shore.

"We did it," Arty cried, gasping for breath. "Sitting Duck is safe!"

Sam's face beamed with pride. On the anniversary of Sitting Duck's founding, they'd managed to save it from catastrophe once again. "Not bad for a bunch of kids!" he yelled as the water lapped against them. "Not bad at all."

CHAPTER THIRTEEN

Sam, Arty, and Phoebe hauled themselves back onto dry land, just by the Sitting Duck Harbor. They pulled Emmie up with them and lay on the cobblestones for a few seconds, catching their breath. Being a hero is a tiring affair, and it's always important to rest afterward.

Phoebe groaned as she pulled a long piece of seaweed out of her hair. "Eww," she cried. "I need a shower, like now!"

Sam, who was used to all manner of smells and until recently had been using anti-zombie deodorant that quite literally smelled like the undead, figured they had more important things to worry about.

"We got rid of Tweedy," Sam said. "But what about the 'curse'? We still have a town full of statues for residents, including Emmie!"

"Eww, I know," said Phoebe. "Like, some of us managed *not* to get ill off that stupid grog. People should really be more considerate."

Arty scratched his chin. "Hold on a minute. You drank that stuff?"

"Yeah," Phoebe said. "At the fair."

"And you didn't get ill?" he asked.

"What does it look like?" she huffed proudly. "No disgusting green spots for me."

"Well, we know it wasn't a real curse," Arty reasoned. "It was just an illness. But somehow Phoebe is uninfected. . . ."

Arty caught a whiff of something coming from Phoebe's direction. Despite being dunked in the dirty water of Sitting Duck, she still smelled of oranges and lemons and cosmetic gunk.

"You don't stink at all," he said. "That's so odd."

"I think you'll find it's not odd," Phoebe said. "I keep myself, like, smelling fresh, you know? Which is more than I can say for you."

Suddenly, Arty pumped his fist in the air. "I've got it!" he shouted.

Sam and Phoebe looked at him curiously.

"We know that the curse was spread by bacteria in the grog, just like Mr. Tweedy said. But

159

it also broke out on the *Silver Mallard* back when Caruthers was captain. But Caruthers didn't get ill—he was fine and dandy when he wrote that letter. . . ."

"So . . . ?" Sam asked.

"So, don't you see a connection? He mentioned eating limes. And Phoebe here is slathered in fruity cosmetics and won't stop talking about juice."

"I do love juice," Phoebe admitted.

"If it's just an illness," Arty finished, "then it can be cured. And I think a simple fruit juice can cure it. Sailors on long journeys often couldn't get hold of fresh fruits, and it's possible that's how the illness has managed to spread."

Sam looked on thoughtfully. "But that would mean all of Sitting Duck has been avoiding healthy food that could have saved them all along."

"Well, yes," Arty replied. "People here live almost exclusively on pie and quadruple burgers."

Phoebe rummaged around in her backpack and pulled out a carton of juice. Glitterpuff jumped off Emmie and shook his body around, trying to get dry.

"Here," she said. "Let's try it on Emmie."

Phoebe put the carton up to Emmie's mouth and tipped it upward, dribbling the juice into her mouth. At first nothing happened, and Emmie remained motionless. But then her eyes flickered and her little fingers twitched. The gray pallor that had completely covered her started to recede, and the little green spots on her face smoothed themselves out.

Sam, Arty, and Phoebe gathered around.

"Emmie!" said Sam. "Are you okay?"

"Can you hear us, Emmie?" asked Arty. "We made it off the ship. . . ."

Emmie stretched out her legs and arms like a flower opening in spring, accidentally knocking Sam in the face. He didn't care. He and Arty gave her a huge hug before filling her in on what she'd missed and how Sitting Duck was saved. Emmie looked thoughtful for a moment. Then, quick as a flash, she punched Sam, and then Arty, in the ribs. Not so accidentally. They doubled over like deflating balloons.

"Heyyy!" Sam shouted. "What was that for?"

"YOU USED ME AS A LIFE RAFT!" she cried angrily.

"Oh, that," said Sam. "But you were very buoyant. . . ."

"I don't care how buoyant I was," she said. "I'm not a ship!"

Arty just laughed. It was good to have the old Emmie back. "Speaking of 'ships,'" he said, "the *Silver Mallard* is no more."

"And now we know how to cure the Sailor's Sleep," Sam continued. "We can put everything back to normal."

"Oh," Emmie muttered. "Even Great Aunt Doris? Because it's been nice and quiet lately without her around. . . ."

"Well, we'll consider it on a case-by-case basis," Arty agreed.

Together, Sam, Arty, Emmie, and Phoebe made their way out of the harbor, determined to reawaken the town's statuesque inhabitants.

Sam knew that saving the day today didn't

guarantee that something wild wouldn't happen tomorrow. But that didn't matter to him. With Arty and Emmie by his side, he was ready to face down whatever Sitting Duck had to throw at him.

He rummaged through his pockets and pulled out a golden coin. On one side was the *Silver Mallard*, riding high on a dramatic wave. On the other, Armitage Caruthers appeared in profile, looking heroic and dashing and charismatic, all at the same time. He flicked it up in the air and caught it again.

"No harm in keeping just one piece of 'cursed' treasure," he laughed to the others. "No harm at all!"

Read them all!

Disaster strikes the town of Sitting Duck again . . . and again . . . and again. . . .

CHAPTER ONE

Sitting Duck was quiet.

I mean, really quiet. Like, have you ever heard a mouse play the drums? No? Well, that's because they're incredibly quiet. They just can't get a proper grip on the drumsticks and they only have tiny little arms, so . . .

Yep. They're quiet.

However, Sitting Duck was even quieter than that. And that was unusual. Because despite Sitting Duck being a boring kind of place, with seriously boring events like the world's largest stare-into-space competition and the watching-paint-dry Olympics taking place every four weeks, some really unusual things had happened.

First there were the zombies. You know, dead people with bad skin coming back to gnaw people's faces in a not-very-friendly way? Then it was the aliens, who were trigger-happy and smelled like a butt blast mixed with a cabbage burp. And then came the evil scientist and the giant robot, both of which made quite a *lot* of noise. So, without all those things destroying the town, things were pretty quiet, let me tell you.

Although, things do tend to change quite quickly in Sitting Duck. For instance:

"Dull, dull, dull!" a voice cried, shattering the quiet. It was as if someone had heard what I was writing and decided to prove me wrong; it sliced the air like a knife through a balloon. And it wasn't just a voice. If you look closely, you'll see that the voice was actually attached to a real-life person.

Hitching up his backpack, Sam Saunders came wandering around the corner. Sam was an all-out good guy and floppy-haired hero champion. Up until recently he'd been saving Sitting Duck from all the noisy threats that came its way *and* leading the town with his general kick-butt nature in the face of danger. But ever since it got quiet—not so much.

"Dull is a good thing," his friend Arty Dorkins said, walking alongside him.

"Yeah," said Emmie Lane, his other best pal. "It wasn't dull recently when we nearly got our heads blown off by a superintelligent robot." She raised an eyebrow in Arty's direction.

"For the love of dogs," said Arty. "Anyone could have made a maniacal robot bent on destruction. It was an honest mistake!"

Emmie grumbled under her breath. She was pretty sure that only big-brained Arty could do something as dumb as that. (To be honest—and I like being honest—I'm on her side. Emmie is tough, and I don't want to argue with her because she will definitely win.)

Sam remembered how fun it was fighting off the killer robot and sighed. They were on the way to school, and there was definitely nothing to be excited about there. As they made their way through Sitting Duck, the sun shining down and the smell of wet paint drifting through the air from this month's paint-drying competition, they passed the main square. Sam looked up and sighed again.

"I want to be more like him," he said, staring at a statue on top of a tall column.

"Really?" Emmie asked. "Made of stone and covered in pigeon poo?"

"Because that can be arranged . . . ," Arty added.

"No!" Sam cried. "Don't you know who that is?"

He pointed up at the statue. It depicted a man on top of a galloping horse, staring out into the distance. He wore a wide-brimmed hat set at a jaunty angle and had a crooked smile that made him look like he was about to tell a joke. He thrust out a sword with one hand, and in the other he held a duck proudly to his chest.

"Armitage Caruthers!" Sam gasped. "The greatest Sitting Ducker ever to live. They say he sailed the seven seas looking for a place to call home—fighting pirates, gorillas, mermaids—all

so he could create our amazing town!"

Arty and Emmie looked at each other and frowned.

"Mermaids?" Emmie asked.

"Yes! Mermaids are evil."

(Just for the record, I can confirm that that's true. I've met one. He stole my lunch money and spent it on tuna. In general, a good rule of thumb is that if it has scales but also talks to you, it's not friendly.)

"Anyway," Sam continued, "the point is, Armitage Caruthers wasn't afraid of *anything*. Not. One. Thing. Just like me. *And* he was always having adventures. When he eventually landed here, he took his trusty duck companion, Albertus, down from his shoulder"—he couldn't afford a parrot—"and sat him on the ground. And thus, Sitting Duck was born!"

Armitage Caruthers
Character Profile

1. Born in England in Ye Olde Days (a specific historical time period of about 400 years ago).

2. Developed a reputation for adventuring when he single-handedly beat the Loch Ness monster in arm wrestling.

3. Showed a flair for piracy early on when he made his brother Barnabus walk the plank for stealing his favorite pair of socks.

4. Earned a reputation for disaster in 1666 when he accidentally left his oven on and started a small fire that burned down half of London.

5. Left England and traveled the eight seas. (Soon there would only be seven, as Caruthers accidentally pulled the plug on one of them.)

6. Was cursed and imprisoned by the Mermaid Queen for impersonating a monkfish, but escaped and set off for the mystical New World.

7. Founded Sitting Duck but never did shake the Mermaid Queen's curse. (I told you they were evil.)

8. Died a hero, defending the town against its first catastrophic event—the Great Octopus Invasion of 1675.

9. Lives on forever in the hearts and minds of Sitting Duckers.

Create a Disaster Survival Kit

What would you put in your own Disaster Survival Kit?

Maybe, like Arty, a Bristly Brain Basher
(aka toilet brush) is all you need to keep
enemies at bay?

Can you invent a more sophisticated form of weaponry
using a toilet roll or an empty cookie tin?

Or do you really just want some sweets and a clean T-shirt?

Pack your bag for the apocalypse and
keep it by the door in case of disaster!

About the Author

R. McGeddon is absolutely sure the world is almost certainly going to end very soon. A strange, reclusive fellow—so reclusive, in fact, that no one has ever seen him, not even his mom—he plots his stories using letters cut from old newspapers and types them up on an encrypted typewriter. It's also believed that he goes by other names, including A. Pocalypse and N. Dov Days, but since no one has ever met him in real life, it's hard to say for sure. One thing we know is when the apocalypse comes, he'll be ready!